so weird

Strangeling

so weird

Strangeling

Created by Tom J. Astle

Adapted by Cathy East Dubowski

Based on the television script
by Brian Nelson

Disney
PRESS

New York

Printed in the United States of America.
First Edition

1 3 5 7 9 10 8 6 4 2

The text for this book is set in 12-point Palatino.

Library of Congress Catalog Card Number: 99-69511
ISBN: 0-7868-1431-4

Visit www.disneybooks.com

Prologue

A note from Fiona.

All through history people have claimed to have supernatural powers. Witches casting spells, sorcerers conjuring up creatures. Were they all fakers, or were some of them the real deal?

And if they really were tapping into something, what was it? I mean, we use the word magic, but what is magic? Is it just some force, like electricity, that makes things happen? Or is it something else? Something alive. Something that might have a mind of its own . . .

You may not believe it, but I had an experience with witches and magic myself not too long ago.

My name is Fiona. It's an old Irish/Celtic name that means "comely" or "fair." But everyone just calls me Fi—that's pronounced "Fee." My dad started that when I was little. It's one of the few special things I've got left to remember him by. He died when I was very young.

My mom likes the nickname Fi because it's different, and being different is one of my mom's goals in life. She and my dad were in a band together when they were young—they were pretty popular, too. After my dad died, Mom tried to do the middle-class mom bit—house in the suburbs, nice reliable nine-to-five job. She even wore a suit to work and volunteered for the PTA. All cool things—but not really my mom's thing, if you know what I mean. She stopped singing. Not even in the shower. Basically, she was miserable.

And then one day she just made up her mind. She needed to sing again.

So now we're back on the road for Mom's "comeback" tour. We travel from town to town on a huge bus, and she mostly performs in small clubs. Maybe you've heard of her: Molly Phillips. Well, if you haven't, just wait. One day she's going to hit it really big, and everybody's going to know her name.

My fifteen-year-old brother, Jack, says Fi is the perfect name for me because it sounds like somebody from another universe. He thinks I'm so weird just because I'm interested in extraterrestrials, UFOs, and paranormal phenomena—you know, like ghosts and ESP and other strange stuff scientists haven't figured out how to explain yet.

Jack only believes in things that he can see right in front of his face—like his score on a Game

Boy or a pizza with the works.

But I think just because you can't see something doesn't mean it doesn't exist, right?

So here's where the magic comes in. Mom had a show in the town where my dad's sister—Aunt Melinda—lives with her two daughters, Maggie and Miranda. We don't get to see them that often, so I was really excited to get the chance to visit. Especially since Aunt Melinda was going to be in a play.

We couldn't go to the actual performance because Mom had her own show to do that night. But we got to do something even better. We got to go to the afternoon dress rehearsal, and we got to go backstage to see all the stuff that goes on behind the scenes of a professional play.

Aunt Melinda was playing a witch in Shakespeare's *Macbeth*. Shakespeare wrote it in the early 1600s to please the new king—King James—who was the patron of his acting company.

King James's native land was Scotland. He was an impatient guy sometimes. And he believed in witches.

So Shakespeare—smart dude—wrote a play about a brave Scottish soldier. And it's full of witches who make predictions about Macbeth's future—including the fact that he'll one day become king of Scotland.

One cool thing I learned is that the play *Macbeth* has a reputation among actors for being unlucky—probably because there's a lot of evil and treachery in the play. Superstitious actors claim that it's bad luck to say the name of the play out loud or quote any of the lines out loud when they're not on the stage rehearsing or performing the play.

Do you believe in curses? Do you believe in bad luck?

I think maybe I do now. Because here's what happened to me. . . .

Chapter One

Fourteen-year-old Fiona Phillips awoke with a start and grabbed her laptop as her bedroom lurched.

A stuffed animal tumbled from its spot on the shelf above her bed. Her suncatcher swayed.

I must have fallen asleep surfing the Web, she thought. Where are we?

Fi quickly got to her knees and looked out her tiny bedroom window. Across a partly filled parking lot she saw a sign that read:

NORTHWEST REPERTORY COMPANY PRESENTS

WILLIAM SHAKESPEARE'S

MACBETH

LIMITED ENGAGEMENT

"Yes! We're here!" she cheered. She shut down her computer, then jumped up and straightened her clothes. She snatched up a brush from her dresser and began to brush out her long reddish-brown hair.

Not many kids have a bedroom on wheels, Fi

thought, as she sat down on the bed to pull on her boots. Her room was closet-sized but cozy and custom built right into the tour bus that carried her mom and the band from one town to the next. It had felt kind of weird at first, but she was quickly getting used to it. And as long as she had her computer, she was at home anywhere.

Fi grabbed the doorknob to leave, then turned back. Gotta do the map, she thought. On her wall was a big map of the United States. She stuck a pin on the map along the highway they were traveling on. She liked keeping track of all the places they were visiting on the tour. They started at Fi's hometown—Hope Springs, Colorado. And they'd hit a dozen or more towns before they were through.

Fi ran to the front of the bus. It had been a long drive and she was eager to get out and stretch her legs.

Irene Bell slipped into the driver's seat that her husband, Ned, had just vacated. Irene looked like a rock star herself, with her shaggy blond hair and jeans. But she was actually Molly's business manager—she booked Molly's shows and made sure all the business ran smoothly. Her husband was head roadie and a tutor for the kids.

Irene put the bus in gear. "Okay, I'm gonna go to the club and make sure the amps are up to spec. I'll be back to pick you guys up before sound check."

"Now, you sure you don't mind me taking a couple hours off?" Ned asked her. He really wanted to see the play since he and the kids were reading it for their latest English assignment.

"Hey, I never get to boss the roadies around," Irene said. "It'll be good for my ego."

"See ya, Irene," Fi said as she started down the steps.

Fi's dark-haired older brother, Jack, shoved past her to be the first one to hit the pavement. His best friend, Clu—Ned and Irene's son—squeezed by, too. "Later, Mom."

Fi waited on the sidewalk for her own mom to climb down. Molly Phillips usually wore jeans and T-shirts—or something really cool for her shows. But today she looked totally different—really pretty, Fi thought. She wore her reddish-brown hair pinned up in a sleek twist. Her dark flowered skirt reached to her ankles, and she'd buttoned a black cashmere sweater on over her turquoise silk shirt. She was even wearing heels! She was really dressed up to see the play.

It must be fun for Mom to watch someone else onstage for a change, Fi thought.

Molly slipped her arm through Fi's and smiled. "Come on, guys. Ten minutes till curtain. Let's go find Melinda."

Together they strolled through the orange-and-yellow leaves swirling across the sidewalk that led to the theater. Fi thought it was neat that they got to slip in the side door, the entrance the actors used. Inside the large theater, the audience area was empty, but the backstage area was packed with people busy with the last-minute details of putting on a play.

A fair damsel in a velvet gown urgently discussed her lines with another women dressed in jeans and a *Shakespeare in Love* T-shirt. A man in a long red cape strode past two stagehands wearing flannel shirts and carrying a huge papier-mâché rock. A witch squeezed past two prop guys who were carrying a velvet throne.

Fi had been in plays at school, but never in anything this elaborate. She was surprised at how many people it took to put on a professional play. Most of the people worked their magic behind the scenes, unseen by the audience.

Fi trailed her mother as she tried to find Aunt

Melinda in the crowd. Fi stepped back as a man walked by pushing a cart loaded with props—things the actors would use in the play: fat half-burned candles on antique-looking candelabras, a wine bottle and silver goblets, a ruby-encrusted crown; a small fake dagger, and a book.

Something in Fi's chest leaped when she caught sight of the book. It was a large book—about the size of a photo album, but at least five or six inches thick. Golden clasps held the thick leather covers together.

Hand-tooled into the front cover was a picture of a strange winged dragon rearing on up its hind legs. Its forked tongue lashed out as if in warning, its long tail snaking around its body. The design looked centuries old. Was it a real book? she wondered. Or a prop specially made for the play? Fi stepped forward for a closer look, but—

"Sorry!" A guy wearing headphones passed through carrying a ladder, and when Fi looked again, the props cart had disappeared between rows of thick black curtains in the wings.

"Excuse me," Fi heard her mother say politely. "I'm looking for my sister-in-law . . . uh, Melinda Campbell?"

People swirled around them like travelers

hurrying to catch their trains. "Um . . . Do you know where the dressing rooms are?" Molly asked. A couple of knights clanked by, their faces hidden by closed metal visors. Molly turned around and tried again. "Excuse me, I'm looking for . . ." A woman wearing a bulky knit sweater and jeans strode past discussing notes on a clipboard with an actress, whose long blue cape swept to the floor.

Molly sighed, dropping her arms to her sides. "I guess you're kind of busy right now . . ." she said to no one in particular.

Clu's eyes lit up as a knight in full armor clanked past. "Dude!" He slapped the guy on the back—clang! "Stellar outfit!"

Beaming, Clu shoved his dark blond hair out of his eyes and turned to Ned. "You know, Dad, I gotta hand it to you. This is definitely the way to go with teaching us culture and stuff. I mean, seeing *Macbeth* performed live is gonna be way better than reading it, you know?"

"Well, actually, it's a dress rehearsal," Ned reminded him. "The real performance is tonight." Ned eyed his son. "And you did read it, right?"

Clu froze for a moment like a kid caught

cheating. Which, of course, Clu would never do—that wasn't his scene at all. Besides, his dad had this totally accurate internal radar for identifying any schoolwork that wasn't totally original. But reading all the assignments on time, well . . . sometimes Clu got a little too distracted by all the cool things to do while traveling with a band on the road. How could some dusty old play written by a guy four hundred years ago compete with the words and music of a modern rock band?

Clu fudged. He had looked at his copy of *Macbeth*. And he'd meant to read it. Yeah, he was gonna read it. Soon. Definitely.

"Oh! Uh . . . totally," Clu told his dad, nodding enthusiastically—and stuffing his hands deep into his pockets to hide the fact that he'd crossed his fingers. He decided on the spur of the moment that just this once a little white lie was the thoughtful way to go—to keep from unnecessarily upsetting his dad. After all, he was going to read the book . . . eventually. "I read it from cover to cover."

Ned raised one eyebrow, but didn't pursue the issue. As he walked away, Clu sighed in relief.

Beside him, a devilish gleam lit Jack's dark

eyes as he muttered, "Yeah, the covers were all you read."

"Shut up, Jack!" Clu whispered out of the corner of his mouth.

Watching the exchange, Fi couldn't believe it. Despite the fact that Clu and her brother frequently acted like total dopes, Fi knew they were both pretty smart guys. Especially Jack. He had a sharp mind for the cold hard facts that teachers seemed to be so obsessed by. But she couldn't believe to what lengths he and Clu would go to avoid doing their schoolwork. Hey, Fi wasn't a saint when it came to schoolwork, and she knew it wasn't always easy to keep up with studies on the road, with all the interruptions they faced every day. Plus, Fi guessed it was probably extra tough for Clu to have his dad be his teacher, too.

But the guys were totally missing the boat here by skipping out on *Macbeth*.

"Clu, *Macbeth* is like the coolest of Shakespeare's plays," Fi told him. She'd looked up *Macbeth* online and discovered all kinds of neat things. She leaned toward the boys and whispered mysteriously, "They say it's cursed, and all kinds of bad things will happen if you say the name of the play out loud."

Jack—totally immune to fantasy, mystery, superstitions, and anything remotely supernatural—rolled his eyes at his sister. "You mean, like you just did," he pointed out.

Fi frowned. Oh, yeah. I guess I did just say it, she thought.

She shivered and crossed her arms over her chest as she looked around the stage where *Macbeth* would soon be performed by the Northwest Repertory Company. In that case, she thought nervously, let's hope this "cursed" business is just an old urban legend cooked up by Will Shakespeare's public relations guy!

Molly rejoined the group, looking totally lost and bewildered. "She's got to be around here somewhere," she said, still searching the crowd for Aunt Melinda's familiar face.

"I wouldn't worry about it too much, Mom," Jack assured her.

Molly looked at him questioningly.

"All we have to do," he explained, "is stand here . . . and they'll find Fi."

Molly laughed.

"Who will?" Clu asked.

Jack rocked back on his heels and said simply, "M and M."

Clu looked even more totally baffled than usual. "M and M?"

Before Jack could say more, a sound like the squeals of fairies split the air.

Chapter Two

Fi braced herself, preparing to be tackled.

The crowd of bustling adults seemed to part as two little girls flew across the stage toward Fi, like arrows seeking their target.

Whump!

Bull's-eye, Fi thought as the two girls threw their arms around her and tried to hug the breath out of her.

It was Melinda's daughters, Maggie and Miranda. Maggie was eight and wore her long dark brown hair pulled back in a ponytail. Seven-year-old Miranda wore her lighter brown hair pulled back from her face, streaming down her back to her waist.

Fi loved her cousins—they were smart and sweet and as interested in the supernatural as she was.

But they were a bit intense. The girls chattered almost constantly—and usually at the same time, which made it nearly impossible for anyone to understand what they were saying.

"Fi! You're here—!"

"Fi! Fi, Fi, Fi! We've been waiting all day for you—"

"Can we sit with you? Mom said we could—"

"And Mom said you were coming and she said we could sit with you and—"

"—but she said we had to not fight and I could sit on the left—"

"And I could sit on the right . . ."

Fi's eyes flicked back and forth between the two girls as she struggled to understand their conversation.

Fi grinned weakly. "Uh, hi, Maggie, hi, Miranda—"

"We just surfed your Web site," Maggie blurted out excitedly.

"Yeah—'Life is so weird'!" Miranda quoted.

Fi had set up her own Web page last fall. It was called:

Fi's

So Weird

Web page

LIFE IS SO WEIRD

The *O* in the word *SO* was an animated cartoon eyeball that moved all the time, like it was looking all over the place, searching for UFOs. That was one of her favorite parts.

Fi had designed her Web site as a place to explore the unexplained mysteries of the universe—things like hauntings, UFOs, and magic. If it was weird, strange, or supernatural, Fi was probably interested in it.

Without taking a breath, Maggie announced, "I believe in ghosts!"

"Me, too," Miranda said. "And they're not scary!"

"They just want help!" Maggie said.

"And aliens aren't mean—" Miranda said, shaking her head with conviction.

"They're just lost," Maggie explained, "and looking for a home—"

"Don't you think?" Miranda asked.

"Don't you?" Maggie asked.

The two sisters finished speaking at exactly the same moment. The sudden silence was startling. They stared up at cousin Fi as if she were a movie star, their eyes shining, waiting for some jewel of wisdom to fall from her lips.

Jack and Molly grinned knowingly.

Clu looked at the two young girls in stunned amazement.

Fi tried to figure out which comment, question, or explanation she should try to answer first. "Um— well . . ." She shrugged and took a shot at it. "I guess!"

That answer seemed to please both girls, and they smiled at each other in delight.

"Come on!" Miranda said as she grabbed Fi's hand. "Mom's waiting!"

"Yeah, come on!" Maggie squealed, grabbing Fi's other hand.

With their favorite cousin between them, Miranda and Maggie ran off, pulling Fi behind them like a helpless kite.

Clu stared, speechless, his mouth hanging open.

"Aunt Melinda's kids," Jack explained. "The twin tornadoes." He chuckled. "They like Fi."

Clu blew his bangs out of his eyes. "Guess so."

Molly, Ned, and Jack all laughed, then Molly put her arms around the boys and tried to follow the quickly disappearing girls.

If they lost them in the crowd, Molly wasn't worried. They could simply follow the trail of the fairylike squeals.

Down in the dressing room beneath the stage, a

witch preened as she sat at a mirrored dressing table dabbing stage makeup on her face. The large round lightbulbs of the makeup mirror illuminated the haggard lines she drew around her eyes and down her cheeks with greasepaint. Her long grayish-brown hair shot out in a boisterous tangle, as if she'd just flown in from a trip on her broomstick through a major storm. As she worked, she mulled over the words of an incantation she would soon recite as she dropped eye of newt and toe of frog into a boiling cauldron of witches' brew.

"Mom! Mom!" Maggie squealed as she ran up to the ugly old witch.

"She's here! She's here!" Miranda announced.

The witch—Molly's sister-in-law, Melinda—turned around and gasped in delight, her cheerful smile sitting oddly on the face of an old hag.

"Molly!" She jumped from her seat and threw her arms open wide.

"Hey, sweetie," Molly said fondly. The two women laughed as they threw their arms around each other and hugged. "Oh, it's so good to see you."

Looking over Molly's shoulder, Melinda spotted Fi and rushed to engulf her in hugs as well. "Fi! I knew the girls would find you!" She stood back and beamed at Fi as she held her at arm's length. "Oh, you're so beautiful! And Jack! Oh, my gosh!" She released Fi and turned toward her nephew, throwing her arms open wide. "Jack—give an old witch a hug, you handsome devil."

"Hey, Aunt Melinda," Jack said with affection, enduring her exuberant hugs good-naturedly.

Fi couldn't help but laugh. It looked funny for a haggard old witch to be hugging a teenage boy with such glee. It's easy to see where Miranda and Maggie get their enthusiasm, she thought with a giggle.

When Melinda released Jack at last, Molly introduced her sister-in-law to her road manager. "Melinda, this is Ned Bell, and his son, Clu."

Melinda eagerly shook the big man's hand. "It's great to finally meet you! Hey, you roadied for Molly and Rick back in the Phillips-Kane Band days, right?"

"My wife and I, we're like barnacles," Ned joked. "We attach ourselves to great talents."

Clu said hello to Melinda, then a startled look crossed his face. "Hey! You're one of the Weird Sisters, right?" In the play they were about to see, the three Weird Sisters were witches who would make prophecies about the future of a brave Scottish warrior named Macbeth. Clu jabbed Jack in the ribs and whispered proudly, "I read that on the back cover."

"I'm the head witch," Melinda said, pretending to brag, fluffing her wild witchy hair. But then she glanced at the clock on the wall and sighed. "And we're going onstage in about five minutes, so I'd better get on my broomstick!" She turned to Molly. "Now, Ron's out of town on business—he was really sorry he missed you guys. . . ." She pulled a dark sleeveless cape from a clothes rack, and Molly helped her slip it on over her bloodred dress. "But the girls will show you where to sit." She laughed and shook her head. "They've been to so many dress rehearsals that they're practically ushers."

Grinning like elves with secrets, Maggie and Miranda each grabbed one of Fi's hands and tugged her toward the stairs that led to the audience seating. They spoke quickly, their voices layering over each other like two different radios blaring at once.

"Yeah, we can show you!" Maggie declared. "It's just a rehearsal, so we can sit anywhere—"

"We can show you where the seats are," Miranda proclaimed proudly, "because we've been here a million times and—"

"—but I'm going to sit on the left and Miranda's going to sit on the right . . ."

"I'm going to sit on the right and Maggie's going to sit on the left. . . ."

Fi just shook her head and let herself be dragged to her seat.

Maggie and Miranda insisted they sit right in the middle of the theater, about twelve rows back from the stage.

"These are the best seats in the house," Miranda told Fi.

"And we should know," Maggie said with a giggle. "We've tried out every one of them."

Fi didn't doubt it, and she agreed the spot the girls had chosen was perfect. She settled down into her seat with Maggie and Miranda on either side of her.

Each continued to chatter away, and seemed not to notice that the other sister was chattering away at the exact same time.

Like stereo bookends, Fi thought dryly. But she had to admit she enjoyed the attention. She didn't have any younger siblings. And having two little girls absolutely adore you was a nice change from getting picked on by a goofy big brother all the time.

Speaking of older brothers . . . her brother, Jack, sat a few rows ahead of her with Clu, and they were practicing their favorite sport—scarfing down unreal amounts of junk food at the speed of light. At least they weren't punctuating it with one of their burping contests!

Fi groaned. The crunch of a big foil bag of potato chips and the slurping noises from paper cups of ice and soda were definitely ruining the mood.

"Hey, Jack!" she called down in a loud whisper. "Can you guys try eating like normal people?"

Jack's only answer was an extra-loud slurp.

Maggie and Miranda giggled, but Fi made a face. "I bet you're not even allowed to eat in here!" she told her brother.

Jack turned around in his seat with a mock expression of indignation. "Why, we're just trying to recreate the full experience of watching a Shakespearean play," he informed her.

Fi made a face. "Say what?"

"Hey, it's true," Jack said, leaning back over his seat. Then he adopted the voice of a very educated professor to add, "I'll have you know that in Shakespeare's time, it was quite the normal thing for roving vendors to sell drinks and snacks to the members of the audience to feast upon during a performance at the Globe Theatre."

Aha, Fi thought with a grin. So my big brother has done some reading after all. The Globe Theatre was where Shakespeare's plays were originally performed in the early 1600s.

"Really?" Clu said, amazed. "You mean, like, the hot dog guy at a baseball game?"

"Exactly," Jack replied. "Besides," he added, "it gives the playgoers something to throw at the stage if the play stinks!"

"Jack, you wouldn't dare!" Fi gasped. "Not Aunt Melinda's play!"

Jack guffawed, delighted to get a rise out of his sister. "Don't worry, Miss Manners," he reassured her. "I promise to behave."

Clu laughed, then glanced up at Ned, who sat in the row behind Fi a few seats over. "So, Dad," he joked, "do we get, like, some extra credit here? You know, for impersonating a Shakespearean audience?"

Ned gave his son a "give me a break" look, then said, "Fi's right, you guys. Keep the munching noise down to a respectable level—or the chips are mine. Got it?"

Clu gave his dad a thumbs-up sign, then twisted back around in his seat. Fi chuckled as she watched him painstakingly try to reach into his bag and pull out a single chip without making the bag rustle.

Jack managed to sip his soda without a single slurp.

Fi looked around the theater, waiting for the play to begin. Later that night, for the real performance, the theater would be packed with people. But for the dress rehearsal the audience was only about a third full, with people scattered evenly throughout the seats.

Excellent, Fi thought. For once there was nobody sitting in front of her to block the view.

She glanced back at her mom, who sat behind her, and whispered, "This is going to be great! I haven't seen Aunt Melinda in a play since I was little!"

Molly nodded. "You're in for a treat. She's really good." Then she placed a finger to her lips. The play was about to begin.

Fi slouched down into her comfortable red velvet seat. The theater was pretty new, and really nice, with luxurious seating and modern lighting equipment. But she tried to imagine what it was like to watch this play when it was first written. Wow, that was nearly four hundred years ago, Fi thought. A lot of TV shows and movies came and went these days, and a lot of kids complained about having to watch reruns on TV in the summer. But Shakespeare's *Macbeth* had continued to capture the imagination of audiences for centuries. She couldn't wait to see it.

At last the dark velvety curtains parted, revealing a dramatic set.

Fi shivered in delight at the spooky scene laid out before her. The lighting manager had bathed the entire stage in an icy blue light. At the left of the stage a huge full moon hung in the air. Eerie white fog snaked around rocks and boulders like a living thing. Long ragged cobwebs fluttered down toward the stage like ghostly fingers.

The three witches writhed and swayed around a waist-high black cauldron shrouded in twisted briars.

The head witch hunched over the boiling, smoking cauldron, her eyes wild with second sight.

I can hardly believe that's Aunt Melinda, Fi thought. She had totally transformed herself with her acting into another person from a different time. The head witch raised an opened book into the air and bellowed her incantation into the night: " 'Round about the cauldron go; In the poisoned entrails throw . . . Fillet of a fenny snake, In the cauldron boil and bake; eye of newt, and toe of frog, Wool of bat, and tongue of dog, Adder's fork, and blindworm's sting, Lizard's leg, and owlet's wing—' "

As she read off the ingredients to her wicked brew, the two other witches tossed in what looked like real entrails and eyes and toes.

Maggie tugged on Fi's sleeve. "See that book Mom's holding?" she whispered.

"Yeah," Fi whispered back and smiled. "I saw it earlier."

Maggie grinned knowingly, then revealed a deep dark secret. "It's a real book of magic spells."

Miranda pressed in from the other side and nodded. "Mom told us so."

"Hey," Fi whispered secretively. "Did I ever tell you guys that witches run in my family?"

The girls' eyes gleamed with excitement as they leaned forward to hear more.

Unfortunately, Fi's mom leaned forward from her seat behind them, too. "Fiona . . ." she drawled, a note of warning in her voice.

Gulp. Fi had forgotten about Mom sitting back there. For some reason, Molly always seemed to disapprove when Fi got too carried away with her talk of the supernatural. Fi wasn't sure why. Well, maybe *disapprove* was too strong a word. It's like my interest worries her for some reason, Fiona thought.

Then again, maybe she just didn't want Fi to fill the young girls' heads with ideas. "Well, uh, that's what Gramma Kathleen says, anyway," Fi told her mom with a chuckle.

"The only thing that runs in our family is noses," Molly said firmly. "Now, let's watch your mom."

The girls obediently turned their attention back to the stage. But Maggie and Miranda beamed with their newfound knowledge that their cousin Fi was a witch!

Fi quickly lost herself in the story again as Aunt Miranda's witchlike cackle filled the auditorium: "'Toad, that under cold stone Days and nights has thirty-one Swelter'd venom, sleeping got, Boil thou first i' th' charmed pot!'" She stirred the pot faster. "'For a charm of pow'rful trouble, like a hell-broth boil and bubble, Double, double, toil and trouble, Fire burn and cauldron bubble!'"

The witch crowed with evil delight as she raised her magic book of spells high above her head.

That's when Fi saw it.

The dragon on the front cover of the brown leather book glowed like magic fire.

Fi stared at it in disbelief.

Then the golden light faded away.

Fi held her breath. She glanced around quickly to see if anyone else had noticed. Was it her imagination? Was it a trick of the props department?

Or was it true what Maggie and Miranda had told her?

Was it a real magic book?

Chapter Three

"**M**elinda? You were terrific!" Backstage after the play, Molly rushed to congratulate her sister-in-law.

"Oh, thank you!" Melinda gushed.

The two started hugging all over again.

Fi chuckled. You'd think Mom and Aunt Melinda would have run out of hugs by now, she thought, but here they go again.

"Brava!" Ned said. "A truly fine performance." He enveloped her in one of his famous bear hugs.

"Well, I guess I'm just naturally spooky," Aunt Melinda said with a giggle.

It was funny, Fi thought, watching her aunt now. Physically she looked the same as she had onstage. Same wild hair, same costume, same ghostly makeup. But she wasn't a witch anymore. She was Fi's funny aunt Melinda. It was the acting, not the costume, that had turned her into a totally different person.

Before the dress rehearsal, the backstage area had been a madhouse. Now most of the cast and crew were slipping out for a bite to eat or to grab a quick rest before the show. Only a few people remained checking lights and putting props back into place for tonight's performance.

"That was so cool," Jack said as he and Clu wandered around the wings, poking around through the props and costumes. "You think they were using real swords?"

"Nah, man, they're all fake," Clu said. "You see, Dad worked on the Kiss reunion tour. They had a bunch of that stuff. What I want to know is—where'd that ghost guy come from?"

Clu's eyes lit up as he spotted a huge metal crank—like something that would wind up thick heavy chains to open a drawbridge. "Yes!" He pounced on it and turned the crank, trying to figure out how it worked.

"Hey! Hey, guys—" Ned rushed over and laid a heavy hand on the crank. "This isn't a playground here."

Aunt Melinda called over one of the stage crew. "Gina, could you take the boys down under the stage? That's where we do all our stagecraft," she explained to Jack and Clu. "Gina can show you some tricks."

"Score!" Clu held out his hands.

Jack slapped his hands. "Awesome!"

Quickly they disappeared down the spiral staircase that led to the rooms below the stage.

"Hey, can I come, too?" Ned asked, and Melinda waved him along.

Then Melinda linked arms with Molly and led her toward the stairs. "Now, come on down to the dressing rooms with me and tell me how brilliant I was. I don't get enough of that around the house."

Molly laughed.

Melinda turned back to her daughters. "And girls? You can stay up here, but do not get underfoot, all right?"

"Okay, Mom," Maggie and Miranda chirped together.

"Bye, honey," Molly told Fi.

As soon as their mothers left, the two young girls surrounded Fi. They pulled clothing off the costume racks and began to dress her up. Maggie tied a long black cape around Fi's shoulders. Miranda plopped a pointed black witch's hat on her head.

Helpless to object, Fi laughed. "What are you guys doing?"

"You're a witch," Maggie stated as she tied the strings of the witch's cape beneath Fi's chin. "So you should wear witch stuff!"

Miranda sighed. "I wish we could be witches, too."

"But we can't," Maggie told her sister firmly, "because we're only cousins and not sisters."

"Yeah," Miranda said sadly.

Fi glanced around. The stage area was deserted now. "You know," she whispered, "witchcraft is a very mysterious thing. It might work for cousins, too."

Miranda's eyes lit up. "You think?"

"Silly!" Maggie said, grinning. "She knows!"

"We could all be witches!" Miranda said, her voice hushed in wonder.

"We could be real-life Weird Sisters!" Maggie exclaimed.

And together they shouted, "Thank you, Fi!" and hugged her as if she'd just granted them some wonderful honor.

Fi laughed, but then her smile faded as something on the stage captured her attention. Staring through the thorny branches that surrounded the witches' cauldron, Fi spotted the book: the magic book Aunt Melinda had used in the play! It was lying unopened on a huge fake rock.

Fi couldn't help herself. She was dying to get a

peek inside that book. She kept thinking about how it had glowed in the play. Was it a real magic book, as Maggie and Miranda claimed? Or just a cleverly made stage prop?

Slowly she walked out onto the dimly lit stage. She glanced down at her hands and arms. They were blue! Soft blue from the blue gels that covered the lights drenched the stage. Thick curtains cast dark shadows into the wings, and the lights in the auditorium had been switched off, so that everything beyond the edge of the stage disappeared. Fi had the feeling of stepping into another world.

At last she reached the rock. Hands trembling with excitement, she reached down and picked up the book.

Whoa! It was heavier than she'd expected. She gazed at the front cover, at the beautiful yet eerie engraving of the mystical dragon. She ran her hand over the indentations in the leather, looking for some sign of trickery or wires or batteries—anything that would explain how Aunt Melinda might have made the cover image glow during the play.

She found nothing.

Fi shrugged. Of course, there could be many

explanations, the commonsense side of her brain reminded her. Someone standing in the wings could have shone some kind of light on the book to get the glowing effect.

But the other side of her brain—the side that believed in all things mystical—wasn't convinced.

Fi unhooked the chunky brass clasps, then opened the book.

The pages were thick and crisp, like parchment. The book had the feel and smell of an old book from the library. Is that what this is, then? she wondered. An old library book? But it seemed too fine and rare. But if that were true, why would Aunt Melinda leave it lying around onstage?

Suddenly Miranda and Maggie appeared at her side. They had dressed themselves up in tall black witch hats and long black capes, now that Fi had declared that they might be witches, too.

They seemed strangely quiet and spoke in hushed tones.

"That's the magic book," Miranda pronounced in a reverent voice.

Maggie pointed to the cover. "It's got a really neat dragon on the cover. See?"

"And real magic spells inside," Miranda added.

Fi studied the book. It was definitely the same

book she'd seen on the prop table when they'd first arrived. The drawing of the dragon looked ancient and mysterious. Viewed from the side, the mythical creature stood upright on its hind legs, as if walking like a human. Its long slender tail curled around its legs like a writhing snake.

"Where'd Aunt Melinda get this thing, anyway?" Fi asked.

Maggie shrugged. "Out of our attic, I think."

The thick yellowed paper rustled as Fi carefully turned the pages. The words were handwritten in beautiful calligraphy with thick black ink. At the top of each page there was a single word written in English, like *Love* or *Warning*. The first letter in the text was drawn in color with an image—such as a lion or griffin—worked into the design. But all the other words on the page were strange, written in a different language.

At last her hand stilled at one page. The title read "Strangeling." The first letter of the text incorporated the image of a dragon—the same dragon that appeared on the cover of the book. Fi studied the words, and even though she couldn't read them, the spelling and accent marks looked familiar.

"Hey, I think this is Gaelic," Fi told her cousins. "It's the language of the Celtic people of

Ireland. My Gramma Kathleen tried to teach me some when I was in Philly."

The girls crowded around her, fascinated. The fact that Fi knew something about the magical words in the book seemed to further establish their belief that she was a real witch.

Footsteps in the wings made the girls look up.

"Talk about Weird Sisters," Jack teased as he strolled onstage and eyed the three girls in their witch wear. "They don't get any weirder than you guys."

Maybe it was the costume Fi was wearing. Maybe it was the way it felt to be standing on the eerie set of a real play. Whatever it was, Fi instantly fell into character. Eyes flashing, she raised her hand and pointed at her brother. "Don't come near me, Jack," she warned in the stern voice of a witch, "or I'll turn you into a frog!"

Jack smothered a grin, but instantly played along, throwing himself into his role for the benefit of his audience of two. "Oh, no!" he squealed, his voice high-pitched like a little boy who was afraid. "Don't do that!"

Maggie and Miranda were delighted by their older cousins' antics.

"Do it! Do it!" Maggie cried gleefully.

"Can you?" Miranda asked, her eyes growing big. "Do you think?"

"Show him what a real witch can do," Maggie begged Fi.

Grinning, Fi opened the huge book of spells again. And again—how weird—the book opened to the page with the word *Strangeling* at the top. For an instant, she paused, her hand resting on the mysterious writing, as a strange sensation washed over her. What was it? Fear? Foreboding? The burritos she had eaten from the drive-through for lunch maybe?

The feeling disappeared as quickly as it had come.

She shook her head. On with the play! she told herself. She grinned at Jack over the cover of the book and gave him a secret wink.

Jack wiggled his eyebrows, signaling that he was ready to play along.

Fi tried to look mean and scary as she turned her eyes back to the ancient words on the page and began to read out loud. Of course, she had absolutely no idea what she was saying. And she was sure Gramma Kathleen would probably cringe at her pronunciation of the Gaelic words. But she figured her speech was good enough to convince her two young cousins that she knew what she was saying—that she was actually casting a spell on her brother.

Holding the book in her left hand, she waved her right hand in the air and crept around the witches' cauldron.

Jack pretended to cower in fear as she circled round him, poking at him and glaring, and did her best to pronounce the ancient words of the book's spell:

"Oon dommen-tall goo jee an dommen saul-ta-see . . . tar-ah bay-tie, tar-ah feedah, tar-ah meestair . . . in annum moon-teer O'Shannon!"

Finally, she thought with a chuckle as she whirled around the stage, my lifelong dream from all those past Halloweens, to play a real witch, comes true! She cackled in delight.

Her cousins giggled.

Jack writhed and groaned as he sank to his knees, pretending to be in agony. "Aaahh! You did it!" he cried out. "You did it!" Then, like a first grader in his first starring role in a school play, he sat on his heels and performed a hilarious impersonation of a frog. "Ribbit—ribbit—"

Maggie and Miranda laughed and clapped their hands in delight.

Fi grinned, pleased that her brother was being cool enough to make a fool of himself for a good cause—that of entertaining his little cousins.

But then suddenly, in the middle of his hopping and croaking, in the middle of his joking around . . .

Something so weird happened.

Fi felt the book lurch in her hands.

She heard a strange rushing sound, like cymbals blended with a muted roar.

And then the book leaped from her hands! It fell to the wooden stage with a loud *WHOMP!*

Fi stared down at the book as it lay open by the toes of her boots. What—? What's going on?

Then—*boom!*—something exploded between her and Jack. She glanced up. But a flash of light blinded her. The smell of smoke stung her nose.

Maggie and Miranda's squeals of delight became terrified screams!

Fi rubbed her eyes and looked around. For a moment, she couldn't move, couldn't make sense out of what had happened.

Thick white smoke turned blue as it floated in the eerie stage light, forming a cottony blue wall between her and her brother.

Jack . . . ?

Trembling, she fanned the air as she stepped through the smoky wall. She gasped as she caught sight of something—something small—as it scuttled off into the shadowy wings.

And when the smoke cleared . . .

Jack had disappeared.

Chapter Four

For a moment nobody spoke.

Then Maggie's voice split the silence. "You did it!" she shrieked. "You're a real witch, Fi! You're a real witch!"

"He turned into a frog!" Miranda shouted at the same time. "You really did it!"

"Whoa, whoa, whoa—hold on, you guys." Fi's heart pounded as she looked around, trying to figure out what had just happened. She stared at the spot where seconds ago her brother had squatted on his heels, acting like a goofy frog.

He wasn't there. He wasn't anywhere onstage.

Fi took a few steps toward the wings. The same direction in which she'd seen something small dash off right after the explosion. But that . . . that thing was far too small to be Jack.

At least, too small to be Jack in his normal form.

"You chanted the spell!" Miranda cried, her fear now replaced with wonder.

Fi turned back and stared at her cousins. What were they thinking? That she had really turned

Jack into a tiny, icky, slimy green frog? Sure, she felt like doing that to him sometimes, especially when they'd been on the road for a long time without a break, but . . .

That was impossible . . . Wasn't it? You couldn't turn your brother into a frog simply by mispronouncing Gaelic words you didn't even understand from a book that was probably a fake stage prop.

Could you?

"Listen, you guys," Fi said, her voice trembling, trying to convince them—trying to convince herself, "it's not a real spell—"

"He turned into a frog and hopped off!" Maggie insisted. Her eyes flashed, challenging Fi to deny it.

"That was *not* a frog!" Fi argued.

Miranda folded her arms across her chest and calmly demanded, "Then what was it?"

"You're a witch!" Maggie cried happily, jumping up and down as if she'd just opened what she'd wished for at a birthday party. "You're a witch! You're a witch! You're a witch!"

Fi yanked the black hat from her head and shouted, "I am not a witch!"

The girls looked startled. Miranda looked as if she might cry.

Fi immediately regretted speaking so harshly to the girls. But things were getting out of hand here. She couldn't let them think that she'd worked magic. . . . She couldn't let them believe the things that were racing through her own mind.

She walked toward them, her hands outstretched. "Maggie . . . Miranda . . ." she said gently but firmly, "there are no such things as witches."

Maggie looked aghast. "How can you say that?" she exclaimed, her hands clutched to her chest. "You!"

"If Jack's not a frog," Miranda demanded, her face as grave as a miniature lawyer, "where is he?" She folded her arms to rest her case, and waited for Fi to explain.

Good question, Fi thought nervously. She turned around slowly, searching the theater. He's here, she told herself. He's hiding. It's just the set that's making us think outrageous things . . . Walking through the set for Macbeth's witches, with a pale full moon behind her, and cobwebs reaching down as if to snatch her away . . . Well, it was a scene that would make anybody's imagination work overtime.

Time to find Jack and put an end to all this foolishness.

"Jack?" she called out tentatively.

No answer.

A shiver ran through her. "Jack!" she cried out, frightened that he didn't answer. Then "JACK!"—angry that he maybe he heard her but wouldn't answer! And in the next minute she was worried. "JACK!" she pleaded. Her voice echoed across the stage.

But no matter how many times she called him, Jack didn't answer. Or couldn't.

"Look for a lily pad!" Miranda suggested with the logic of young girl who still believed in fairy tales. "Frogs live on lily pads!"

"Yeah," Fi muttered under her breath, "I'm sure the theater is full of lily pads."

Something rustled overhead.

Fi whirled around.

Then the sound darted through the drapes and valances hanging above them along the curtain line. A sound like the flapping of wings. Dry leathery wings.

Fi peered up into the jumble of ropes, pulleys, and lighting equipment usually hidden from the audience by the curtains—and thought she saw something. Something flying above them, like a bird, or . . . something else. A large hunk of a shape in flight. Something too large to be any bird she'd ever seen.

Fi shivered the way she had the time Jack dumped a cup of ice down her back, but she forced herself to step forward, her head tilted back, searching through all the clutter hanging above them for a glimpse of whatever was up there.

She gasped as a dark shape swooped from one shadow to the next, wings flapping.

"What is it? What is it?" Miranda cried.

"Did you see him?" Maggie gasped.

"I think I saw his shadow!" Miranda exclaimed.

Fi didn't answer. She wasn't sure what she'd seen, but she knew in her heart that the dark fluttering shape was definitely not a bird.

It can't be Jack, either, she thought. Or at least, it couldn't be her big brother in the body he normally walked around in.

A wave of horror washed over her. What have I done?

Could it be? Had she really magically changed Jack into something?

Fi broke out in a cold sweat. She was a smart girl with a good head on her shoulders, but she believed in the supernatural too much to dismiss what others would find impossible. She was scared, really scared. She wanted nothing more than to run out of the theater, climb into the bus, lock the door to her tiny closet of a room, jump into her warm cozy bed, and pull the covers up over her head. And stay there till she woke up from this horrible nightmare.

But it wasn't a nightmare. It was real. Horribly real. And it was all her fault.

Then she gave herself a mental shake. Get over it! she told herself. Quit whining and do something about it!

She had to follow the rustling sounds. She had to find out what was really going on. She had to find out what had happened to her brother!

Then she remembered her two young cousins. She could feel them staring at her back, waiting expectantly. They trusted her. Looked up to her. Believed anything she said. And, Fi hoped, would do whatever she told them.

She wasn't sure what she was looking for. But if somehow Fi had truly conjured some magic here, it might be dangerous. Better if Maggie and Miranda aren't around, she thought.

Slowly Fi turned around. Her heart was

pounding and her trembling hands threatened to give her away. But she balled them into tight fists and forced herself to smile at her cousins, as if they were playing a game. Now, *that's* acting, she told herself.

She gathered the girls around her, then went down on one knee so she could look them straight in the eye. Struggling to keep her voice calm and playful, she whispered, "Okay, listen. If we're going to find Jack, we'll need to split up."

The girls grinned, thrilled to be included in Fi's magical adventure.

"I want you guys to go look down in the dressing room, but—" She glanced around, then leaned in to whisper, "Don't tell anyone what we saw, okay?" She forced a chuckle. "I mean, if Mom finds out I turned Jack into a frog, I'll be in such big trouble. Okay?"

The girls nodded with enthusiasm.

"It's a secret!" Miranda declared happily.

"I knew something weird would happen when you came," Maggie said, beaming in adoration. "Yay!"

"Okay, hurry!" Fi said, still forcing a smile as she shooed them toward the stairs. "Hurry, you guys. Go on, scoot!"

The girls dashed off like little fairies on a mission for their queen. They giggled all the way down the stairs that led to the dressing rooms.

Fi's smile faded as she rose to her feet. She took a deep breath. Then she began her search. Her search for her missing brother . . .

Who might—thanks to her—be a frog.

Chapter Five

The only sound in the entire theater now seemed to be the echo of Fi's boot heels on the wooden stage. She didn't hear anything move, couldn't hear the rustle of those wings.

Not so long ago the backstage area had been a bright, exciting place, a virtual circus of people dashing about as they readied costumes, sets, and lights for the play.

Deserted now, it was a place full of shadows and secrets. Downright spooky. With hundreds of dark places for . . . something . . . to hide.

"Jack?" she called out as she looked around the stage. "Jack, where are you?"

The silence frightened her. "Jack . . . ?"

She climbed up the spiral staircase that led to the catwalk—a narrow, bridgelike walkway that allowed the stage crew to pass above the stage, unseen by the audience. From here, they could raise and lower background scenery, manipulate lights, make the world below behave as they directed.

Fi wished she could control what was happening so easily.

I probably shouldn't be up here, she thought as she reached the top and stepped out onto the catwalk. But she felt the presence of something up here, waiting, watching. Carefully she walked along, peering into the tangled world of ropes, pulleys, lumber, and wires.

Whatever she was searching for could be anywhere.

Something fluttered behind her. A tiny sound, but in the silent theater it seemed to fill Fi's ears.

Tingling with fear, she turned around and followed the sound . . . step by cautious step . . . trying not to make a sound herself.

At last she reached the end of the catwalk. She looked down.

Whoa! The broad wooden stage lay a long way down. Her stomach lurched, and she tore her eyes away. Don't look down, she told herself. You'll be fine if you just don't look down!

Then she heard a different sound. Just beyond her. A sound like a slobbery growl.

Fi's mouth went dry. "Jack?" she managed to gasp.

She peered into the gloom.

A long horizontal metal pipe hung from the ceiling by thick ropes. The pipe swayed slightly.

Something was on it—there! Near the end. A dark shape. Something alive, watching her.

Fi gulped and took a tiny step forward. "Jack?"

No answer.

"Jack, I know that's not you . . ." she said nervously. "But, well . . . if it is you, I don't know . . . chirp or something!"

The dark blob sitting in the shadows inched backward. Its heavy breathing sounded wet and hot. Like a big rabid dog.

Dogs don't climb up to the ceiling of theaters, Fi assured herself.

"Jaaaack. Please! I didn't mean to do this," Fi wailed. "I mean, I didn't do this," she insisted. Then doubt crept into her voice. "But if I did, I'll make it up to you. I promise. Okay? So just please come back . . . Please?"

Jack—or whatever it was—growled softly.

Maybe he's hurt, Fi thought. Or scared. Or confused. If it was Jack, he had to be totally freaked out to suddenly find himself turned into something else.

This is all my fault! Fi thought frantically. I have to do something!

She could hear the creature's heavy, wet

breathing as she stepped closer. When she reached the railing of the catwalk, she bent down and slipped between the bars. Carefully she reached out for the metal pipe with one hand. If she could grab hold of it, and pull it, swinging it toward her on its ropes, maybe she could reach the creature who hovered in the shadows on the other end.

If it was Jack, she would talk to it. Convince it—him—that she was there to help. Somehow.

She pulled the pipe toward her. It moved easily, swinging toward her.

But one hand wasn't enough. Bracing herself carefully against the catwalk railing, she reached out with both hands.

She grabbed the end of the metal tube and pulled.

Flap! Flap! Flap! The creature startled, and suddenly took flight.

Frightened, Fi shrieked and lost her balance.

She was going to fall!

Chapter Six

Something grabbed her. She hung in midair.

Fi screamed again.

Was it the creature?

Don't scream! her mind shouted at her. It might drop you! She closed her eyes against the vision of the stage that loomed up at her from far below.

"Fi!" a gruff voice thundered.

Crying out in relief, Fi realized that the large hands that gripped her belonged to Ned Bell. His strong arms encircled her and dragged her back onto the catwalk, saving her from a tragic fall.

"Ned!" Fi threw her arms around his neck and clung to him. Silent tears streamed down her face as she tried not to imagine what would have happened to her if he hadn't been there to save her.

"Oh, baby. It's all right," he said, hugging her tight, patting her on the back. "It's all right now. I've got you."

He held her till she stopped shaking. He dried her tears with a red bandanna. Then, when he was sure she was okay, he helped her climb back down the spiral stairs to the stage.

"You see, it's my fault, Fi," he said as he led her back to the spot on the stage where Jack had disappeared. Where she might have landed a few minutes ago if she'd fallen.

"You see, I was telling the boys about trapdoors and flashpots," Ned was saying. "You know, the way they make Banquo's ghost disappear in the play?" He shook his head. "Jack said he was just going to show you."

Fi frowned. What was he talking about?

Ned reached down and picked up a small trigger mechanism attached to the end of an electrical cord. The long cord led over to small fake rock. And behind that fake rock was what Ned called a flashpot—a small metal cylinder sticking up out of the floor. It was about twelve inches tall and about as round as a dinner plate.

What does this have to do with my fall? she wondered.

On the floor in between Fi and the flashpot Ned also pointed out the outlines of a trapdoor.

"Okay, now, see here?" Ned held up the trigger mechanism. "When I open the trapdoor, that triggers the flashpot."

He pushed the button with his thumb.

Whomp! Fire and smoke instantly exploded

from the flashpot. At the same time the hinged trapdoor fell open.

Now I get it! thought Fi. She could see that the flashpot–trapdoor combination was a perfect device for allowing a ghost or other character to quickly disappear from the stage without being seen. The audience's eyes would be drawn to the flash of fire. The smoke would shield the exit of the ghost.

Or . . . the sneaky brother.

Now Fi understood what had really happened earlier when she had read the spell from the magic book. Her toad of a brother hadn't turned into a frog or anything else. He'd simply dropped down through the open trapdoor, making his escape while well hidden behind the harmless flash and smoke of the flashpot.

Fi leaned over and stared down through the trapdoor into the dressing room below.

Guess who? Fi thought wryly.

Jack and Clu stared up at her. They wore knight's armor and foolish grins. Jack tried to look innocent.

Ned turned back to Fi. "When I heard they were planning to trick you, I came looking for you." He leaned down over the open trapdoor

and shook his finger at the boys. "Hey, guys—
NOT COOL!"

"Sorry, Mr. B.," Jack said sheepishly.

"Sorry, Dad," Clu mumbled.

Ned shook his head and got to his feet. "I'm
going downstairs," he told Fi. "Please, Fi—stay
off the catwalk."

"Thanks, Mr. B.," Fi said softly.

She waited till Ned had left, then glared down
through the trapdoor at her brother. How embar-
rassing! She'd almost killed herself running after
some strange winged monster that didn't even
exist—and all the while Jack had been laughing at
her. How humiliating! "Oh, really funny, Jack!"
she shouted. "I almost broke my neck looking for
you! You know," she added, "I wasn't fooled by
that bird-monster thing for a second!"

Clu stared at her with a puzzled look on his
face. "Bird-monster thing?" He rocked back on his
heels and grinned. "Cool!"

But Jack looked at her as if she had spoken to
him in Polish. "What are you talking about?"

Fi couldn't believe it. He'd been caught red-
handed, his prank totally revealed. And he still
thought he could play dumb? "Fine!" Fi shouted.
"Act like you don't have a clue. It won't take

much talent!" She shook her head in disgust, then walked away.

She was so mad at her brother! He was always playing stupid tricks on her like this. This was almost as bad as the fake alien message he'd once sent her on the Internet. She still blushed when she thought about it. She'd been so excited! She was convinced that she was getting a message about a real UFO sighting. But when she logged on to her So Weird Web site, she'd found a computerized picture of Jack, saying, "Take me to your leader! Take me to your leader!" in a goofy alien voice.

I can't believe I was dumb enough to fall for this one, she thought. A book with spells that turned brothers into frogs. A growly, slobbery monster with wings. You'd think I'd learn!

A slow deep growl stopped her in her tracks.

Fi slowly turned around and glared into the shadows. "Cut it out, Jack," she warned. Did he think she was so stupid she'd fall for another joke so soon?

Snarl!

Fi froze. The hair stood up on the back of her neck.

The sound had come from a part of the backstage area that was in front of her. But she'd just seen Jack and Clu downstairs, through the trap-door behind her. And they were wearing suits of armor. Could they have gotten all the way up here in just a few seconds? No way, Fi thought. At least, not without her hearing them clank.

The noise over there . . . it couldn't be Jack.

She knew her mom and Aunt Melinda were still down in her dressing room chatting. The cast and crew had mostly cleared out for a break before the show tonight. Besides, none of those people were likely to growl at her.

Maggie and Miranda would make a whole lot more noise creeping up on her. And she didn't think they would ever try to scare her. They liked her too much. And they were way too sweet.

Fi licked her lips. "Uh . . . hello?"

No one answered back.

It was a lot easier to believe that everything that had happened to her this afternoon was just part of Jack's stupid prank.

But then she remembered the look on his face when she'd yelled at him about the "bird-monster thing." How he'd said, "What are you talking about?" as if he really didn't have any idea what she was talking about.

Maybe he didn't.

But something was definitely there. Waiting for her in the shadows. She could feel it staring at her. She could smell something . . . something dank and slimy.

Was it the same thing she'd glimpsed up on the catwalk?

Somehow, deep inside, she knew that it was.

That creature wasn't part of Jack's lame joke.

The creature was real!

Another growl—like a soft warning, from a creature that knew it didn't have to shout to be listened to.

Then the growl faded to a damp, heavy breathing. The sound seemed to surround her as she stood there, alone, trying to decide what to do.

Fi knew she'd have to face it. Hey, it's not like I can slip away without it noticing, she thought. She could feel its penetrating stare in the middle of her back.

Maybe it's some kind of hawk or falcon, she tried to convince herself. Yeah—that's it! Some large, wild game bird they planned to use in the play. But maybe it got loose and so they couldn't use it at the dress rehearsal, and now everybody's out looking for it and . . .

She knew she was grasping at straws. And as scared as she was, Fi wasn't the kind of girl to sit and wait to be rescued. She had to do something. Now.

Slowly, very slowly, so as not to startle the . . . whatever it was . . . Fi turned around.

Then froze in terror.

The scream caught in her throat—like a scream in a nightmare.

Only Fi wasn't dreaming. This nightmare was real!

Staring back at her was a living, breathing dragon!

Chapter Seven

Fi wanted to run. She wanted to run and not stop till she was in the next county!

But she couldn't move. Her feet felt glued to the floor. Her hands froze at her sides.

Absolute terror will do that to you.

She waited for the dragon to pounce on her and devour her in one bite. She hoped it would all be over fast. "Bye, Mom. Bye, Jack," she whispered silently, her lips barely moving. She closed her eyes. She hoped Maggie and Miranda would remember her fondly.

A few seconds passed. Nothing happened. The dragon didn't attack. Fi opened her eyes.

The dragon cocked its wrinkled green head and looked at her with slanted red eyes. It drooled from a mouth filled with sharp, needlelike teeth.

Fi relaxed a fraction, but still didn't move. Maybe he wasn't going to devour her on the spot. Maybe she'd have a chance to fight—or flee. She remembered something her father had taught her as a young girl—what to do if she was ever faced with a vicious dog. Stand still, don't run, don't stare into its eyes, and never, ever show fear. Then slowly walk away, as if you own the neighborhood.

Easy enough to do with a poodle, Fi thought.

As terrified as she was, a tiny part of her was fascinated. How many people had ever had the chance to stare into the eyes of a real, live dragon? She studied it as she waited for it to act. It was smaller than she'd expected, about the size of a big dog. But she had no doubt its sharp, needlelike teeth and monstrous claws would be lethal in an attack. Its green skin looked like ancient leather, wrinkled by centuries of movement. Small horns jutted up from the top of its head, and a large set of batlike wings sprouted from its back.

Suddenly it growled at Fi and raised its wings to take flight.

Fi ducked. She covered her face and head with her arms as she heard the flapping, felt the wings brush her hair.

And then it was gone. It had disappeared once more into the dark recesses of the theater.

Fi sucked in a huge draft of air. She must have been holding her breath. She glanced around the theater.

She couldn't hear the dragon anywhere, but she knew it was out there, somewhere. Sooner or later it was going to hurt someone, she worried.

Then a thought hit her: I did this. I summoned this dragon somehow by reading those ancient words from Aunt Melinda's magic book.

I've got to stop it.

Somehow . . . before it's too late . . .

Fi sat on a big fake rock and opened the magic book. Maybe there was something in the book— something that would help her figure out what to do. How to make the dragon go away.

Maggie and Miranda hovered around her, peppering her with questions.

"So you turned Jack back from being a frog?" Miranda asked.

"It wasn't a frog," Maggie told her sister. "It was a . . . dragon thing."

"And it wasn't Jack," Fi added.

With each word, their girls' voices grew more excited, as if they were thrilled to be part of some game. They were still young, and they spent hours watching their mother move easily between the roles in her plays and real life. Maggie and Miranda believed in magic with all their heart, but it was an innocent magic, the magic of a fairy tale.

Fi had once believed in simple magic like that. Magic fairy tales with witches and dragons and handsome princes. Fairy tales with happy endings.

But she knew that this magic was real. And they weren't guaranteed a happy ending.

"What did it look like?" Miranda asked her.

"Where did it come from?" Maggie said.

Miranda's eyes gleamed. "Did you make it with the spell from the magic book?"

"I don't know!" Fi said, slamming the book in frustration.

The smiles on the girls' faces died instantly.

Fi could have kicked herself. She didn't mean to yell at her cousins. They were just little kids. They hadn't seen the dragon. They had no idea how serious this all was.

"I'm sorry, you guys," she said softly. "I . . ."

Fi never finished her sentence. She glanced down at the cover of the book she'd slammed closed. Her mouth fell open in surprise. She couldn't believe what she saw. Couldn't believe she hadn't noticed it when she picked up the book.

Something strange was going on.

Something really strange.

The picture of the strangeling that once graced the cover of the book . . . the image that had been hand tooled into the thick dark leather hundreds of years ago . . . the picture that Maggie had pointed out to her earlier this afternoon . . .

It was gone.

That can't be, Fi thought. She flipped the book over in case she'd gotten mixed up.

No dragon there either.

Fi turned the book back over and ran her fingertips over the front cover. She felt only smooth leather where the engraving of the dragon should have been.

It couldn't be.

But it was true.

Fi stared up at her cousins in amazement. "The dragon," she said in a hushed voice. "It came out of the book!"

Chapter Eight

"**H**ey, these things are made of plastic!" Jack exclaimed.

He and Clu were goofing around in the costume room below the stage. They had both tried on breastplates over their regular clothes and were looking for weapons to match. Jack pulled a broadsword out of a pile of miscellaneous junk. It looked awesome, like something a real knight would carry into battle. Only it was totally fake.

Clu slashed through the air with a curved plastic sword. "Told you, man."

Jack didn't care. This stuff was totally cool anyway. The small room was packed with all kinds of props and costumes from dozens of plays. Suits of armor in every size lined the walls. Several clothes racks held everything from medieval gowns to miniskirts to Santa suits. Bins were stuffed full of swords and canes and flags. Shelves were piled high with fake weapons, some really cool fur hats with horns, old-fashioned lamps, and birdcages. Jack even dug up an old football trophy. Wonder what play they used that in?

Clu stopped fighting an imaginary foe and turned to Jack. "Hey, Fi seemed kinda like she was mad at you."

Jack shrugged as he lifted up a helmet that looked as if it would fit him. "Ah, comes with the territory. When you're a big brother, you can't do anything right."

"I don't know about that, man," Clu said. He laid down his plastic weapon to slip a helmet on over his head. "I mean, Carey is my big brother," he went on, his voice muffled by the helmet, "and he is the coolest."

Jack pulled on a helmet, then paused. "So what are you saying?" he said. A challenge. He turned and flipped down the visor. "There's something wrong with me?"

"Of course not, Sir Jack!" Clu replied through the breathing holes in his helmet. "Except for the fact that you are e-vil!"

"You insult me, scoundrel!" Jack retorted.

"Well, then," Clu said, turning behind him to grab the hilt of a plastic sword, "I suppose we shall fight about it!" He whirled back around to face Jack, his broadsword raised in an unmistakable invitation to fight.

Jack raised his voice—and his own plastic

sword. "You'll eat those words!" he cried.

"I'll eat vegetables first!" Clu growled in reply.

Grunts and groans filled the air as the two knights fell upon each other in a playful battle that would have made a real audience laugh.

Meanwhile, Fi and her cousins hurried across the stage toward the wings. As Maggie and Miranda pulled off their witch hats, Fi took the book from Maggie's arms.

"Okay, shhh," Fi whispered. "We have to try to get this . . . dragon thing back in the book before everybody shows up for the performance tonight, okay?"

"Okay," both girls answered softly.

For once Maggie and Miranda weren't chattering at ninety miles an hour. Their voices were hushed, as if they realized serious things were about to happen.

The three girls stopped in front of a door with the word PROPS painted on the frosted-glass window. A soft light glowed from within.

Fi looked at her cousins. "Shh."

The girls nodded, then Fi turned toward the door. She laid her hand on the cool brass doorknob, then slowly turned. The heavy wooden door squealed on its hinges as she pulled it open.

Afraid to go forward, yet knowing she must, Fi forced herself to step over the threshold. Maggie and Miranda clung to her sides, and they all moved forward together, like a string of paper dolls.

The room was filled with a dusty jumble of props used in dozens of past plays: old posters, rolled-up scenery, faded Oriental rugs. Old-fashioned telephones, a treasure chest, framed pictures, and junk. It reminded Fi of the time her mom had piled everything up in the garage for a yard sale.

At the far end of the small dark room a small amount of soft light glowed through a colorful stained-glass window. Two full suits of armor stood guard on either side.

And there—something sat on a table between them!

Fi quietly grabbed her cousins' hands. "Look," she whispered.

A black shape sat silhouetted against the colored glass of the window. It was about the right size, but it was as still as a statue.

The girls peered at the shape, trying to see in the dim light.

"Is that it?" Maggie whispered.

Fi squinted. She thought she saw pointed ears, vague shapes at the side that could be wings. But she wasn't sure. "I can't tell."

Miranda moved forward. "I'll find out."

But Fi held her back.

"No!" Maggie warned her sister. "It could bite . . ." Her eyes widened in fear. "It could breathe fire!"

"Wow," Fi said. She hadn't even thought of that. "It could."

"What if it tries to scorch us?" Miranda asked.

"At least the scenery's fireproofed," Maggie joked nervously.

But no one laughed—they were too scared!

Fi inched forward, and the girls copied her tiny steps. But what could they do when they got to it? Fi wondered. She had to think of something. Some way to capture the creature till she could figure out how to send it back into the book.

Fi glanced around the piles of junk in the prop room, searching for something to use. A cage, maybe. Or a bag. Or some kind of rope.

There! Over in one corner Fi spotted some loosely woven burlap fabric. She hurried over and picked up a piece—it was about the size of a bedsheet and surprisingly heavy. "Maybe we could use this as a net," she whispered to the girls.

Holding the fabric in front of her, she walked toward the dragon, which still sat on the work-table before the stained-glass window. "Here, little dragonthing . . ." she called softly.

The dragon answered with a low menacing growl.

Fi forced herself to take another step forward. "Now be a good little, uh, mythical creature, and get back in the book."

Step by step, closer she crept.

Then she saw its face clearly for the very first time.

Ugh! Its leathery dark-green skin looked a thousand years old. Its eyes glowed like red-hot coals. It growled, drooling foul goo as it bared its long, sharp teeth. Inside its mouth its tongue and gums were the color of blood.

Fi's whole body shook in fear as she took another step forward, holding out the net. Keep going, she told herself. One more step . . . almost there . . . almost—

The dragon roared. Its wings shot out.

Maggie and Miranda screamed as the dragon flew straight at Fi's face!

Chapter Nine

Fi gasped and ducked. She waited for dragon claws to gouge her skin.

Maggie and Miranda screamed and huddled together against the wall.

Fi felt the wind of the dragon's flapping wings as it soared above her, barely missing her head.

She jumped to her feet as Maggie and Miranda ran to join her. She looked around, searching the shadows for the dragon, but she didn't see it anywhere. "Where did it go?"

They heard its wings rustling in the shadows. Heard its deep, raspy breathing. Felt its eyes watching them, waiting.

Then Miranda shouted, "There! In the corner!"

The dragon growled and spread its wings.

Oh, great! Fi thought. Now it's between us and the door. We're trapped.

Fi felt a tiny tug on her sleeve. It was Maggie, still clutching her mother's book. "Maybe there's something in the magic book," she whispered.

"Right!" Fi said. "Like a counterspell!" She took the book from Maggie's arms and carried it over to a table. In the dim light from the window, she flipped quickly through the pages.

"It's all in that funny language," Miranda said worriedly.

"Strangeling . . ." Fi muttered as she searched for the page she had read from before. At last she found it. The small painted drawing of a red dragon entwined itself around the embellished *O* of the first word of the spell. She stared at the words, their meaning still a complete mystery to her.

"Read it again," Maggie suggested urgently. "Maybe that will undo the spell."

"Or bring another one here—with our luck," Fi said.

"What else can we do?" Miranda said.

Desperately Fi tried to think of another way. Perhaps they could hide and wait for someone to find them. But who knew how long that would take? What if no one found them until . . . until it was too late?

Fi couldn't just sit and wait. She had her cousins' safety to consider as well as her own. I have to take a chance on the magic book, she thought. Oh—if only I'd listened when Gramma Kathleen tried to teach me Gaelic!

Fi summoned all her courage and lifted the

heavy book into her arms. "Wait here," she whispered to her cousins.

Then slowly, slowly she stepped forward, reading aloud the strange words once more: "Oon dommen-tall goo jee an dommen saul-ta-see . . ." she began. She followed along beneath the words with her finger, so in her nervousness she wouldn't miss a word and ruin the spell. ". . . tar-ah bay-tie, tar-ah feedah, tar-ah meestair . . ."

The dragon bared its dripping teeth, warning her with an ominous growl.

Fi trembled from head to toe, but would not turn away. Bravely she raised her voice as she spoke the final words of the spell: ". . . in annum moon-teer O'Shannon!"

The strangeling cocked its head for a moment, as if considering Fi's words. Its eyes drooped. Fi wondered if it was falling asleep!

Then lightning flashed! The dragon growled angrily.

Something was happening!

The spell—it was working!

The girls gasped, terrified but hopeful, as the dragon roared, its leathery skin crackling as it twisted and turned. As if in agony, the creature raised up on its hind legs. It stretched its wings—

wings that seemed to grow bigger and bigger.

Lightning flashed. Thunder rolled. The dragon growled and arched toward the ceiling. Skin ripped and bone cracked as the dragon seemed to hatch out of its own skin.

Fi's heart sank. Yes, the spell was working. But she realized it wasn't making the dragon go away.

"It's getting bigger!" Maggie cried.

Fi slowly stepped in front of her cousins, who were frozen to the spot, terrified.

The dragon roared and spread its wings, growing, growing, till it loomed over the girls, at least ten feet tall.

Fi felt Maggie trembling against her arm. "Fi," she breathed, "do we look like dinner?"

Chapter Ten

Down in the dressing room beneath the stage, Aunt Melinda was slowly changing from a witch back into a mom. She pulled off her heavy tangled wig and brushed out her own short brown hair.

"It's Fi, Fi, Fi, Fi, Fi, Fi, Fi, Fi," she told Molly and Ned who stood behind her, watching the transformation. "She's all they've talked about for two weeks."

Ned chuckled. "I'm guessing that would be a lot of talking, huh?"

"The only break I get," Melinda confided with a grin, "is when they're visiting that Web site of hers." She got up and crossed to the wardrobe rack to remove her cloak. "Well, I do hope that you like them, Molly," she joked. "Because I think they'll be moving in with you as soon as they save up bus fare."

Molly grinned. "Well, that's great! We can always use a couple of tiny little roadies."

Melinda turned and smiled at her sister-in-law, with her hands planted on her hips. "It's funny that Fi is into all that weird stuff, isn't it?"

Molly's smile faded, and she looked away.

Melinda stared at her sister-in-law in amazement. "You mean . . . you haven't told her?"

Ned frowned and glanced back and forth between the two women. A moment ago he'd been laughing and talking and enjoying the jokes. But now suddenly he had absolutely no idea what they were talking about. He was just about to ask what he'd missed when—

Crash! Jack and Clu burst into the room fighting. Their plastic swords flashed as they clowned around.

"What ho, knave!" Jack shouted.

"That's Mr. Knave to you!" Clu replied.

"You dare to challenge me, varlet?" Jack exclaimed in mock horror. "Take this!"

Jack lunged at Clu.

Just in time Clu dodged the thrust, but knocked some stage makeup onto the floor.

"Whoa, whoa, you guys!" Molly stepped between the two warring knights and grabbed the blades of their plastic swords. "This is a no-jousting zone," she declared.

"Oh." Jack straightened his helmet, then raised his blade toward the door. "Onward!" he cried.

Clu bravely followed, shouting, "Out, out, darn spot!"

Molly and Melinda laughed as they watched the boys thrust and parry their way out the door.

But when Molly turned back, she found her sister-in-law staring at her, with folded arms.

Molly hated that look. She knew it well. It was Melinda telling her that she hadn't done something she was supposed to. Something she knew she should.

But this . . . this secret they shared . . .

Molly wasn't ready to tell Fi yet.

She didn't know if she'd ever be ready.

Chapter Eleven

I've got to get the girls out of here, Fi thought.

Maggie and Miranda were so scared they were speechless. The dragon now towered above them, its roar like thunder, its thick skin oozing green slime. Its red eyes flashed above terrifying jaws.

Somehow she'd have to distract the dragon so her cousins could escape. Maybe then they could run for help.

"Okay, Maggie, Miranda—when I tell you guys, I want you to run out that door!"

"But, Fi—" Miranda protested

"Miranda," Maggie said firmly, tugging on her sister's arm. "She's the witch. She knows how to take care of this."

Maggie looked worried, but she nodded her head in agreement.

Fi glanced back at the dragon and shivered. It was licking its lips. Not a good sign! "Okay," Fi said quickly. "When I count three. One . . . two . . . three!"

The girls ducked and darted for the door.

At the same time Fi grabbed the magic book from the table and rushed at the dragon, trying to draw its attention away from the girls. She held the magic book up in front of her face like a shield.

The dragon roared as it twisted its head back and forth between Fi and her cousins.

The little girls screamed!

It seemed like forever to Fi, but at last the girls reached the door. They turned back toward Fi, their eyes full of anguish. They didn't want to leave her!

But they had to—it was their only chance! "Guys!" Fi shouted over the dragon's roars. "Shut the door. Shut the door!"

With one last look, Maggie and Miranda slipped out and slammed the door behind them.

The dragon growled at the door for a moment. Then it whipped back around, its eyes trained on Fi.

Up on the catwalk, high above the stage, Sir Jack and Sir Clu continued their historic battle. They were evenly matched, and both vowed to fight to the end—or at least until their plastic swords broke.

"This castle isn't big enough for the both of us!" Clu shouted. "Take that, you varmint!"

"Ah!"

"Ugh!"

"Oof!"

Suddenly Miranda and Maggie ran up the stairs. But the boys ignored them. They were too busy fighting to deal with ladies-in-waiting.

"Jack! Clu!" Maggie shouted. "Fi's in the scene shop and she's fighting a dragon and you have to go save her! Hurry! Hurry!"

Jack and Clu exchanged a grin. Then Jack flipped open his visor and raised a gloved finger in the air. "Hey!" he proclaimed in a knightly voice. "We do dragons!"

But the girls didn't laugh.

"We're not kidding, Jack!" Miranda shouted.

"It's a real dragon," Maggie insisted, "with wings and big scary teeth!"

Jack rolled his eyes and sighed. "Okay, okay," he said in his normal voice. He and Clu would have to finish their contest later.

Jack lowered his sword and bowed to his friend. "I'll go rescue the damsel in distress. Sir Clu, you stay here and guard my cousins while I . . . sally forth into the fray!"

"Right!" Clu replied. "It is a far, far better thing you do than . . ." He couldn't remember the rest of the words, so he ended with "than you usually do. Ha, ha, ha!"

Jack gave his friend a strange look. He really did need to study a little more. That misquoted line wasn't Shakespeare. It didn't have anything to do with knights and dragons. It was from Charles Dickens's *A Tale of Two Cities*, a book about the French Revolution.

I'll have to lend him my copy, Jack thought.

He waved farewell to Sir Clu, then, with great ceremony, marched toward his cousins.

Hmm, that was weird. . . . He'd never seen M and M act so serious before. Or be so quiet. They looked totally scared! Jack chuckled. Fi must be doing an awesome job with this little fantasy of hers. Maybe she'd inherited some of Aunt Melinda's acting talent.

"Be careful, Jack." Maggie sounded worried. "Really!"

"No sweat," Jack replied. He flipped down his visor, raised his plastic broadsword, and aimed it toward the stairs. "Uh, I mean—*en garde!*"

"Good luck, Sir Jack!" Clu cheered.

With a mighty shout, as if going off to do battle for King Arthur himself, Jack marched off to save his sister in distress.

Down in the prop room, Fi clutched the magic book to her chest, took a deep breath—

Then made a mad dash for the door. She darted around an old trunk, her long dark hair and witch cape streaming out behind her. . . .

Then the dragon roared and leaped to block the door, like a dog guarding a bone.

Okay, so the dragon doesn't want me to leave, Fi thought.

She was terrified. But she had to get out. And from her encounters with the supernatural, she'd learned one thing. Courage didn't mean you weren't scared. True courage meant you acted brave in spite of being scared.

So she gathered her courage, took a deep breath to calm herself, then tried to speak to the dragon in a brave voice: "Listen, strangeling. I don't know if you speak English. But you don't want to stay in this world." As she spoke, she held up the book and inched toward the door. "I mean it's noisy. And you'll get hit by helicopters when you try to fly. I mean, what are you going to eat? Kids these days—we're full of junk food." She laughed nervously. "So we won't even taste good!"

The dragon lunged at her as if to take a bite right there and prove her theory wrong.

Fi screamed and stumbled to her knees, holding the book up like a shield.

Great, Fi told herself. Make him think about food!

She expected the dragon to strike her, but suddenly it veered off. The sound was chilling, like the wings of giant vampire bats.

Fi got to her feet wondering why she hadn't been singed by the dragon's fiery breath, or devoured by its giant teeth. She looked around. Where had it gone? She spotted the dragon sitting on a high storage loft, hissing as it glared at her.

Hmm, Fi thought. There was a pattern here. Several times the dragon had moved to attack her, then changed its mind at the last minute. What could it be? What was he scared of?

"It's the book!" Fi suddenly realized. "That's it, isn't it?" Her mouth curved up in a slow grin. "You just don't want to go near the book. . . ."

She tested her theory by jabbing the book toward the dragon.

The creature jerked backward, growling its dislike.

Fi nearly laughed out loud. She was pretty proud of herself for figuring it all out.

Then she noticed the dragon moving. What was it doing?

Fi gasped. The creature was using its talons to push over a couple of tall walls of painted scenery that had been stacked against some shelves.

Scenery that was ready to crash down on Fi's head!

Chapter Twelve

She shrieked and sprinted toward the door. She could feel the wind made by the large scenery flats as they fell to the floor. They crashed just inches behind her.

Fi didn't look back. She just kept running till she was out the door.

Maybe she could find Jack, or Clu, or Ned, or her mom. Anybody. She had to stop the dragon before somebody got hurt!

As Fi ran for the stage, she heard the sound of her brother's footsteps coming toward her from offstage on the other side. Then she saw him. When he got to center stage, he paused and made a dramatic pose, as if he'd just made a grand entrance in a play. "What ho, sis!" he called out. "I hear you're in distress!" He made a pretty good knight, especially wearing the costume armor. But he could have picked a better time to put on a show.

"Jack!" Fi screamed, running right by him on the stage.

Jack looked around. Fi could tell he was

having trouble seeing out the narrow eye-slit of the helmet. The blue light that still lit the stage didn't help much, either. Everything seemed dark and shadowy.

Fi held out the book, and the flying creature banked and swooped around again. It thumped into Jack, spinning him around as it flew into the rafters.

"Hey, watch it!" Jack griped as he stumbled. When he stopped spinning, he asked. "Wh-what was that?"

Crouching on the stage, Fi looked over the book at her brother. "That wasn't me, Jack," she informed him in a shaky voice.

"Oh! Right." Jack chuckled. "It was 'the dragon,'" he said sarcastically.

Fi looked around. She didn't see or hear the dragon anywhere now. But she could sense it hiding up there, somewhere, in the darkness. "I don't know what it is," Fi murmured. "But it's dangerous."

Jack held up his shield and took a few wild swings, slashing his sword left and right in the air. But it was impossible to see anything while wearing a visor in the dim stage light. He dropped the chivalrous tone in his voice for a moment and shouted up toward the catwalk, "Hey, Sir Clu! Could you get some lights down here, please?"

Clu jumped to his feet. "Uh, yeah, man, Sir Jack! I'm on it." He pulled off his visor and hurried over to find the switch to the bright follow spot—the overhead light that would send a bright focused beam of light directly where Jack was standing. "Don't worry, girls," Clu told Maggie and Miranda. "I always run the follow spot whenever my dad gets the flu. Okay." He rubbed his hands together, then scampered up a ladder to the catwalk and flicked a switch.

Instantly a bright narrow spotlight hit Sir Jack right in the face.

"Light's up, Jack!" Clu called.

Jack grimaced and held his arm up in front of his face to shield his eyes. "I noticed," he grumbled. The spotlight was blinding, like someone shining his car headlights right in your face. "How can anybody see with those things on?" he muttered.

Fi was wandering around the stage, searching the curtains and wings, looking for the dragon. She couldn't see it anywhere, but thanks to the good acoustics of the stage, she could hear its raspy breathing.

"Jack," she said at last. "We need to get some help!"

"Fear not, my annoying sibling!" Jack cried, whirling around, following her voice. Fi was as invisible to him as the dragon was to her. "I'm here to rescue thou, or . . . whatever." He looked like a knight playing blindman's bluff.

Suddenly—out of nowhere—the dragon roared and plunged toward Fi. She wailed and held up the book, using it like a shield to block the attack. Frightened by the book, the dragon veered past Jack, spinning him like a turnstile, then ducked away to a hiding place in the wings.

"Huh? Hey! What was that?" Jack said, laughing a little uncertainly now as he whirled around. He came to a stop facing Fi, with his back to the dragon. "Is there a cat in here or something?"

Fi could see the dragon's dripping jaws just a couple of feet behind Jack. She started to shout at him, to warn him to watch out, duck, run, hide, something—

Then she stopped. She peered curiously through the blue shadows at the face of the dragon. It was definitely scary-looking. If this were a creature feature they were making instead of Shakespeare, it would easily win an Oscar for Best

Monster. But now the dragon was just sitting there, as if frozen. Frozen . . . and cowering. Frozen with fear!

But what did it have to be afraid of? Fi wondered. The dragon's jaws and claws were deadly weapons. The fire-breather's incendiary breath was powerful enough to level a city with a single puff. Hey, the oversize lizard was big enough now to vanquish human enemies just by sitting on them! No way could it be afraid of two measly kids from the Midwest.

Fi didn't think it could be the magic book upsetting it right now, either. She and the book were on the opposite end of the stage.

Something else is upsetting this dude right now, Fi thought. But what?

Then it dawned on her, and she would have laughed if *she* weren't so scared. How many fairy tales and novels of fantasy had she read in her life? And whenever there was a dragon, who was it that always saved the day?

Who was it that struck fear into the heart of every dragon?

Chapter Thirteen

"**J**ack!" Fi called to her brother. "It's afraid of you! It thinks you're a real knight!"

Jack put his hands on his hips. "Hey, I'm as real as your dragon!"

"Yay, Sir Jack!" Miranda shouted from the catwalk. "Fight the dragon!"

Jack spun around and gazed up to receive the praise from his adoring public.

"You can do it, Cousin Jack!" Maggie cheered. "It's afraid of you!"

Jack chuckled and turned back to Fi. He raised his plastic sword in the air. "Okay, sis," he said with a wink, "let's slay this sucker so we can go get some dinner!"

Fi shook her head. Obviously Jack still thought the whole thing was just a game. He just couldn't see the dragon. The helmet of his costume restricted his view. And the bright spotlight hitting his eyes had surely caused his pupils to contract, making it even more difficult to perceive a dark dragon hovering in the shadowy wings of the dimly lit stage.

But there's something else, as well, she realized. Jack can't see the dragon because he doesn't believe in dragons. He's not even open to the remotest possibility that a dragon could be real. And so he doesn't see a real dragon that's right here on stage, even though it's practically breathing down his neck.

That was the difference between them, Fi thought. Jack closed the door and pulled the blinds against any supernatural experience. Whereas something in Fi—she wasn't sure what—made her look and listen for things that might be.

Fi shook her head. Jack thinks I'm still putting on a show for Maggie and Miranda!

She looked around. Granted, in a way, it almost felt as if she and Jack were in a play. Jack's armor and sword looked right at home on the set of *Macbeth*. The full moon hung behind them in the eerie blue light. Fi could be one of the witches with her black cape and book of spells.

If only she could drop the curtain and put an end to this tale.

But the story was still being written. And the ending depended on the choices and actions Fi alone would make.

If only I could make Jack see that the dragon is real, she thought.

She opened her mouth to try to convince him—

Jack did a little tap dance on the stage as he slashed his sword playfully at a dragon he would never believe in.

Never mind. Fi took a deep breath. Maybe it didn't matter if Jack believed or not. Jack was Jack. But maybe she could still use him to help her get rid of the dragon.

"I have an idea," she told her brother.

She placed the thick book of magic on the floor. Using the side of her foot, she shoved it across the stage like a shuffleboard disc. It spun past a puzzled Jack and came to rest a foot or two behind the dragon.

The dragon recoiled from the book and roared its disapproval.

Jack leaped around and instinctively held up his sword. "Hey! What was that?"

Fi could see she would have to shout instructions to her brother. "To the right, Jack! Go to the right!"

Jack poked and jabbed his blade in the air to his left.

"No Jack! Your other right!" Fi screamed.

Stumbling blindly, Jack swung and slashed his sword in the other direction.

The dragon growled and hissed as it backed away from the knight's attack.

"Go right now, no—left. You're on the left!"

"Left ho!" With each slash of Jack's sword, the dragon growled and hissed angrily, but it also took a step back. And with each step back, away from Jack, it stepped back closer and closer to the book that lay on the floor behind it.

"Straight ahead, Jack!" Fi screamed above the roar. "Swing your sword, Jack! Swing it!"

Jack threw his strength into one air-splitting downward slice. Then he made one well-aimed jab, entirely by accident.

The furious dragon stumbled back.

And stepped onto the book.

And then something astounding happened.

Lightning flashed!

A sparkling light erupted around the dragon, almost like the glittery crackle from a fireworks display. Like the fireworks from the stage flash-pots.

But this was no theatrical trickery.

Sparkling gold rays of light shot upward from

the cover of the magic book and netted the dragon in their threadlike beams. The dragon twisted and struggled, roaring its protest against the light's powerful control. But it was trapped, unable to escape.

And then—Fi gasped in wonder at the sight—the dragon's image transformed into a million tiny points of sparkling light.

And with one final roar of furious protest, the dragon was sucked into the cover of the magic book.

Then all was quiet. The light disappeared. The book of magic lay on the dusty floor like a forgotten library book.

Fi stared openmouthed, trying to absorb all that she'd seen, amazed at having been witness to such an incredible sight.

Fi inhaled sharply and relaxed for the first time since . . . well, since the dragon had come out of the book.

Her only regret was the fact that Maggie, Miranda, and Clu had missed the whole thing. From their vantage point on the catwalk, the dragon fight at the edge of the stage had been hidden from view.

Whomp! Whomp! Slash!

Fi almost laughed. She realized her clueless brother was still slashing away at the air. He'd seen nothing. He didn't realize the imaginary dragon he thought he'd been fighting was a real one. So he didn't realize it was gone.

But hey, it didn't really matter, Fi supposed. Her brother, Sir Jack the Knight, had slain the fearsome dragon all the same.

All's well that ends well! she thought—a quote from the Shakespearean play of the same name. Ned would be pleased that I remembered that!

Fi ran over to her brother and clapped him on the back. He stopped fighting and slid his sword into the holder on the back of his shield. Then he pulled off his helmet, breathing hard from battle.

Fi grinned. Fighting dragons was very aerobic.

"Whew!" Jack said, wiping perspiration from his brow. "Those were some good dragon noises, sis."

Grinning, Fi just shook her head. No way could she have made dragon sounds that real. But Jack would believe what he wanted to believe.

"Yeah, well, that was some pretty good sword-play!" Fi exclaimed. And then—she couldn't help herself—she threw her arms around Jack and gave him a big kiss on the cheek. Brother or not, he had been her knight in shining armor this day, and she couldn't have saved the world without him. "Thanks for the rescue, bro."

Jack grinned, blushed a little, then wiped the sis-kiss germs off on his shoulder.

Squeals erupted in the wings, and Fi and Jack whirled around. Maggie and Miranda!

I guess Sir Jack had better prepare himself to endure a little more adoration from the ladies, Fi thought with a grin.

The girls flew onto the stage, with Sir Clu struggling to keep up with them. The "twin tornadoes" were back in full force, and they exploded with high praise for Jack's great deeds, both talking at the same time:

"He did it!" Maggie squealed. "He did it!"

"You did it, Jack!" Miranda gushed. "It was like—"

"He slayed the dragon! He was so brave!"

"—you were a real knight and everything!"

Jack grinned at the admiration and made an elaborate courtly bow.

Maybe Jack's inherited some of Aunt Melinda's flair for the stage, too, Fi thought with a smile. Laughter bubbled up inside of her—she was just so thankful to have the whole nightmare over.

Should I tell him? she wondered as she watched Jack describe his fighting style to Clu in elaborate detail. Should I tell him he defeated a real dragon? And would he even believe me if I did?

But before anyone could say any more, her mom's voice rang out in the now quiet theater: "What in the world is going on up here?"

Chapter Fourteen

Three very worried grown-ups—Molly, Aunt Melinda, and Ned—came rushing upstairs and onto the stage.

I wondered when they were going to notice something was going on, Fi thought with a grin.

"What was that noise?" Molly exclaimed in that strange mixture of anger and fear that only mother's voice can adequately express.

Aunt Melinda quickly flipped a switch, blinding the kids for a moment with a bright white light that banished all sense of fantasy.

"You guys haven't been playing around with the soundboard, have you?" Ned asked sternly.

Maggie and Miranda shook their heads, practically jumping up and down with the fabulous story they had to tell.

"It was the dragon!" Miranda exclaimed.

Melinda just looked at them. "Dragon?" She laughed. "There's no dragon in *Macbeth*."

Maggie shook her head. "Fi said a spell from the magic book," she explained, "and the dragon came out of the thing on the cover!"

The three grown-ups exchanged glances. Fi could just imagine what they were thinking.

Ned noticed the oversize volume lying on the stage and leaned over to pick it up. He studied the cover a moment, then said, "You mean this thing?" He held out the heavy leather book. The book with the dragon on the cover.

What? Fi gasped. She took the book from Ned and examined the cover. The dragon—the strangeling—was back! The ancient engraving appeared once more in its original spot on the cover of the magic book, walking on its hind legs, flicking its forked tongue. Exactly as it had been before. It looked as if it had never been gone.

Magic!

Fi grinned. She wasn't exactly sure what magic was—it was one of those things that was hard to define. But she was sure she'd seen the evidence of its power here today. And she realized that perhaps she alone had truly seen the magic that had occurred on this stage.

The grown-ups would never believe it. Jack . . . not a chance. Clu . . . he was open to weird things, but he had to see them to believe them. And he was often looking the other way.

And Maggie and Miranda? Well, they believed

in magic in their own way, the same way they still believed in fairy tales and pixie dust.

"But it's true!" Miranda insisted. "It was out, and now . . ." Fi heard the note of doubt creep into her cousin's voice as she realized the grown-ups didn't believe her. ". . . now it's back in," Miranda ended somberly.

Aunt Melinda leaned down till she was eye to eye with her two daughters. "In a dark theater everything seems real," she said with a kind smile. "That's what's so wonderful about it."

The girls responded with matching pouts. It was not the answer they wanted to hear.

Fi knew the feeling. A lot of weird things had happened to her since she'd come on tour with her mom, traveling to new cities, exploring mysteries and strange phenomena. Things she'd witnessed that no one else believed. Fi knew her mom believed in her . . . even when she couldn't quite believe some of the things Fi told her. And Fi had decided that that was good enough for her. For now.

Fi opened the pages of the magic book, studying the writing. Wondering what other secrets the ancient pages held.

"Aunt Melinda," she asked, carefully turning

the pages, "where did this book come from?"

"That?" Aunt Melinda looked surprised by the question. She dropped her gaze, and hesitated, as if weighing what answer she should give. Then she took a deep breath, folded her arms, and said casually, "Your . . . dad dropped it off at our house . . . years ago."

Fi's eyes lit up. This wondrous book had belonged to her dad? Now it seemed more magical than ever. How strange that he had owned a book like this. Maybe I inherited my interest in weird stuff from him, she thought as she turned a page with reverence. Her mom certainly tried hard enough to steer her away from it. Could Dad read this Gaelic? she wondered. Did he understand what all these words meant? Did he ever see any of the magic?

Melinda's smile turned wistful as she watched Fi embrace the book. "It's a beauty, isn't it?" she said softly.

Fi nodded. She admired the cover, where the strangeling once again posed, frozen in mid-snarl. Maybe Aunt Melinda would let me borrow it sometime, she was thinking. Maybe Gramma Kathleen could help me translate some of it . . . and together we could figure out what it all means.

With her eyes on the book, Fi didn't notice the strange expression that crossed her mother's face like a cloud on a summer day. If she had, she might have asked her why talk of the book made her so uncomfortable.

"You know," Aunt Melinda said slowly, watching Fi, "I could use something else for the play." She bit her lip and ignored the pointed glances Molly was sending her way. "Would you like to have it?" she asked Fi.

Fi looked up in surprise. Aunt Melinda was a mind reader! But oh, how could her aunt give up something so cool? "Wow . . . " she breathed. "Are you sure?"

Aunt Melinda nodded.

Fi shrugged. "Well, then—yeah!" She clutched the book as if she couldn't believe it was hers, really hers! It was such a wonderful gift, especially now that she knew it had once belonged to her dad. "Thanks, Aunt Melinda."

Her aunt just smiled.

But Fi's mom did not smile. In fact, Molly seemed stunned by the gift. She shot her sister-in-law another stern look. A look that seemed to say, "Melinda, what are you doing?"

Melinda returned her gaze evenly, without

backing down, her half smile tinged with sadness.

Molly's jaw tightened. Then she looked away and quickly chanced the subject. "Irene'll be picking us up soon," she said with forced cheerfulness. "You guys ready for dinner?"

The two knights in shining armor turned to each other, as if Jack's mom had said the magic words. Grins sprang to their faces. And then together they shouted, "Fiesta Taco!"

Ned rolled his eyes, and Molly threw up her hands in exasperation. "Everywhere we go . . ."

Aunt Melinda grinned. "Come on. I'll show you knights where to hang your armor."

Clu and Jack beat her to the stairs, with Ned close behind. Aunt Melinda and Molly slipped their arms around each other as they followed.

"Hey, Mom?" Fi called after her. She held the magic book open at the "Strangeling" page.

Melinda headed on down the stairs as Molly turned back. "Yeah, baby?" she said softly.

"What was Gramma Kathleen's maiden name?"

A half smile tugged at Molly's lips. "O'Shannon."

Fi held her breath. She ran her trembling fingers down the handwritten page, scanning the lines of the spell she had chanted that afternoon. She stopped when her fingertips came to rest on the final word:

"O Sianhan"—the Celtic spelling of the family name "O'Shannon."

"Why?" Molly asked. She gazed at Fi as only a mother can do, with a look that encompassed a strange mix of love and sadness, hope and fear. As if she were looking through a veil into the future. Or into the past.

"Oh . . ." Fi shrugged and gave her mother an innocent smile. "No reason."

For a moment, dark brown eyes of mother and daughter clashed—and held—over secrets kept and questions unanswered.

What is it? Fi wondered. Why do I get the feeling that she knows something she's not telling me?

Then suddenly her mother smiled brightly. "Coming?" she said. "I'm starving!" She turned and quickly headed toward the stairs.

And Fi wondered if she'd imagined it all.

"Yeah," Fi said softly. She closed the book and took one more look at the dragon.

The book was full of magic, Fi knew. But she also sensed that it held a secret, maybe an answer to some of her questions. Maybe it could even tell her things about her father that she never knew.

She closed the heavy book and hugged it to her chest as she hurried after her mom.

She couldn't wait till tonight. Couldn't wait to curl up in her room with this book and read it from cover to cover.

FROM Web Sight

A note from Fiona:

Have you ever wished you could see the future?

I have. It might be nice to know, when you went to sleep at night, what you were going to wake up to the next day. Maybe it would give you a chance to prepare for it. For me, I don't even know where I'm going to wake up in the morning. I might go to sleep in Ohio and wake up in Maryland. No, I'm not regularly abducted by aliens. I just live on a bus—a tour bus.

My mom is Molly Phillips. She used to be a rock star with my dad in the Phillips-Kane band before I was born. My dad died when I was a baby and mom tried to retire but rock and roll is in her blood. One day she sat my brother and me down in the kitchen and said she was thinking of going back to the music world. She said it would mean leaving our house in Hope Springs, Colorado, and going on the road. She told us to think about it and give her our honest opinions. It was hard leaving everything behind, but we've never looked back.

I think this is what Mom was put on earth to do—it's like her destiny or something. I wonder what my destiny is. Are we all put on earth for a reason? How do we find out what our purpose is?

For the last year my mom's been on a comeback tour and my brother Jack and I get to come along for the ride, which is pretty cool. My mom might be a rising star, but she's my mom first. We all stick together since my dad died. Sometimes my mom says she can feel my dad watching over us. That would be great. Sometimes you need someone looking out for you. If my dad ever sends me a message, I'm sure I'll recognize it because I always keep my mind open and I've seen a lot of weird stuff. We travel around the country with my mom's business managers, Ned and Irene Bell and their son Clu. Clu and Jack share the room next to mine on the bus. We never know what's going to happen when we get to a new town. Like I said, it can get a little weird— luckily, I'm into things that are weird.

I have my own Web site, "Fi's So Weird Web page," where I collect information about UFO's, ghosts, Bigfoot and other paranormal stuff. My brother Jack thinks it's all in my imagination. He thinks nothing happens that can't be explained in an ordinary way. But I can tell you, there's a lot that we don't know about the world and I'm not the only person who wants to find out about it. That's why I have my site—it's for people who have experienced something weird and need to know there's other people out there like them. People looking for the truth.

As long as there's been a tomorrow, people have been obsessed with trying to see it before it becomes today. Nostradamus, the famous French physician who wrote a book of prophecies in 1555, thought he could see the future and a lot of people still believe he could. Others have tried looking at tea leaves, crystal balls, Ouija™ boards, even the palms of their hands.

For those with the "sight," the simplest things can be used to tell what's to come. Even a laptop could be a doorway to the future. But even if we knew for sure what was going to happen, the question is: what would we do about it? I had to answer that exact question when my mom got a gig in a small Maryland town called Dillon.

Dillon didn't seem like the kind of place you'd expect anything strange to happen. But I've learned in my paranormal investigations that the most normal looking towns often have the weird-est things going on in them. That was sure true this time.

We hadn't pulled into Dillon yet, but someone seemed to know what was going to happen when we got there and whoever it was wanted me to know it too.

I didn't know it yet, but things were about to get so weird. . . .

The oversized tour bus with MP painted across the sides drove down a dark highway toward Maryland. The driver, Ned Bell, was a big burly roadie with a bushy red beard and wire-rimmed glasses. He kept his eyes fixed on the road in front of him and easily guided it around a turn. His wife, Irene, sat at a table in a large mobile living room looking over an account book while her friend Molly Phillips strummed her guitar and sang on the couch. A loud thump followed by the loud laughter of two teenaged boys came from another room. "What's going on in there?" Irene called.

"Nothing Mom," her son, Clu, answered.

"Everything's under control," added Jack, Molly's fifteen-year-old son. Molly and Irene exchanged knowing mother smiles.

In another room next to the boys, at the back of the bus, fourteen-year-old Fi Phillips closed her laptop computer and got into bed with a cup of fennel twig tea. She wore a comfortable T-shirt and flannel pajama bottoms. The tea was a special brew that her mom made with loose tea leaves. Molly said it relaxed her after a concert and gave her good dreams. Other people's moms drank ordinary tea out of tea bags they bought at the store, but Fi's mom was different. But then, she was a rock star. They are supposed to be different.

Fi opened up a copy of *The Dillon Dispatch*, a local paper from the town where her mom would be playing the next night. A woman named Susan, who was the calendar events editor, had sent an early edition so that they could see the big ad for Molly's show on page 4. Fi looked at the picture of her mother in the paper. She was holding a microphone and her head was thrown back so her hair fell over her shoulders. She wore a cool leopard-print shirt and a short black skirt. The ad read: *Molly Phillips performing live at the Paramount*

Dance Club this Friday only. It was just a little club, but Molly took every job seriously and gave it her all. That was why she was gaining fans wherever she went.

"Go, Mom," Fi said, taking a sip of tea and putting the cup down next to the silver-headed alien puppet beside her bed. "What's this?" Fi's eye fell on the horoscope page in the newspaper. Her brother Jack thought horoscopes were just made up and would never listen to anything she said, but Fi checked it anyway. "Things are going your way," Fi read. "Of course they are," she said to herself. Jack was fifteen and confident. He was always sure his way was right. Sometimes it drove Fi a little crazy. Just once she wanted to hear him tell her she was right and he was wrong. That probably wasn't going to happen any time soon, she thought.

Fi checked her own horoscope. "Be prepared for danger and you may avert it," she read. "It's all up to you."

"What does that mean?" Fi said, frowning and tucking her long brown hair behind her ears. "How can I keep us out of danger? Ned drives the bus, Irene books the shows, Mom plays the music, Jack's the big brother and Clu— well, Clu just goes his own way. How can I be the one to save them from danger? And what danger could they need me to save them from?"

Still thinking, Fi swallowed the last of her tea. She noticed some loose leaves stuck to the bottom. She had heard that some people read tea leaves to see the future. Fi squinted into the bottom of her cup, searching it with her dark brown eyes. All she saw were three glops of wet leaves that didn't look like anything. One did look a little bit like the tour bus, long and thin, if you turned the cup the right way, and then there was a smaller blob next to it. The third blob hung above the other two like a rain cloud. "Well, that did a lot of good," said Fi. "I don't know anything more than I did before. I already knew we were on a bus without seeing it in a teacup." She heard a soft knock on her bedroom door. "Come in."

Molly Phillips opened the door. She was wearing jeans and a cotton knit sweater. She almost didn't look old enough to be Fi's mom. Some people thought Molly was Fi's big sister. But even though she looked like a big sister, she'd come into the room as Mom. "Lights out, baby," Molly said with a smile. "We'll be getting into Dillon early tomorrow and you've got school with Ned before the show." As well as being a bus driver and chief roadie for the Molly Phillips band, Ned tutored all the kids and kept them up to speed on their schoolwork. Fi was taking the same classes as her old friends back in Hope Springs, Colorado. If she ever went home again, she could go right back to school.

"Mom, did you see your ad in the *Dillon Dispatch*?" asked Fi, holding up the paper. Molly sat down on Fi's bed to have a look. When she saw the ad, her brow creased with worry.

"Maybe I should have worn the green blouse for that picture," Molly said uncertainly.

"Mom, you look great," said Fi. "The leopard print is really cool. You always look really cool." It always surprised Fi that her mom didn't seem to know how cool she was.

Molly smiled and gave Fi a hug. "Thanks kid, I needed that," she said. Then she noticed the horoscopes. "Hey, what's my future?"

Fi frowned suddenly under her brown bangs. "Mine was so weird," she said. "My horoscope says we're going to run into danger and I'm the only one who can save us."

Molly raised her eyebrows. "Sounds pretty serious," she said. "But I can't think of another person I'd rather have doing the saving. You always come through, Fi. It's part of who you are."

Fi laughed and shook her head. Her mom was probably just being nice. "If you say so. What's your horoscope say?"

Molly looked back down the page. "Mine says, don't let the past get in the way of the future. Well, I have no intention of letting that happen. What do you think?"

Fi shook her head. She didn't like the way Mom's horoscope sounded. How could the past get in the way of the future? "I wonder if the danger comes from the past."

Molly smiled at her daughter. She knew Fi was into the paranormal, but sometimes she worried that she got a little too carried away. "Honey, these horoscopes aren't real. They're just a fun thing they print to sell papers. They don't really tell the future. You can't buy into it and let it upset you."

Fi shrugged. She was used to people not believing in the weird stuff that she often felt was all around them. "People have believed in prophecy for a really long time. Much longer than newspaper horoscopes have been around. I invited people to submit stories about people seeing the future on my Web site. Some of them go back to ancient times."

Molly could sense that this was important to her daughter so she took it seriously. "Do you really believe people can see the future?" Molly asked thoughtfully. "I mean, if something hasn't happened yet, how can you see it?"

Fi thought for a moment. "Maybe everything happens for a reason, Mom," she said. "If we knew the reason, maybe we could see what was going to happen. And we'd know why things happened." Fi's voice got very quiet. "Even bad things." Fi saw a look of sadness come over her mom's face for a moment and she knew she was thinking about her dad. It didn't seem fair that he had to die and leave them. What could possibly be the reason for that?

Molly put her arm around Fi and looked into her eyes. "Fi, I know things have been hard for you, losing your dad so young and going on the road far away from home following your mom's dream. But I feel like this is something I should do. I don't know if it's going to work out the way I want, but I have to try. None of us know what's going to happen. We have to take a chance. That's life."

Fi nodded quietly. "It'll work out, Mom," she said. "You're going to be a star." Fi reached behind her and grabbed her teacup. "I read it in my tea leaves, see?" she said, smiling.

Molly laughed, happy that her daughter's mood had lightened. "Well, in that case," she said, taking the cup. "Time for bed!" Molly tucked Fi under the covers and kissed her good-night. Then she kissed the silver-headed alien puppet.

"Pleasant dreams, earthling," said the puppet in Fi's alien voice. Molly turned out the light and closed the door. Fi looked up at the glow-in-the-dark star stickers on her ceiling and wondered what astrologers saw when they looked up into the stars. Was the future really written in the con-stellations, like a blueprint for life? And if the future was already written in the stars, was there any hope that it could be changed? Fi wondered about it until the sound of the wheels on the road lulled her to sleep.

Hours later, Fi lay sleeping in her bed, her left foot poking out from underneath the covers. On the desk across the room, beside a framed photo-graph of Fi as a baby in her dad's arms, her laptop suddenly beeped into life. All by itself the black cover raised up slowly, revealing Fi's So Weird

Web page and casting an eerie glow over the room. "Logging on," the electronic voice announced.

The menu page on Fi's site had a list of links: weird stories, weird pictures, weird sounds, paranormal links and a message board. Fi's dark room was filled with the soft sounds of her modem logging itself on to the Internet; first the sound of Touch-Tone dialing, followed by the crackling and hissing of the modem making a connection. The visitor counter on Fi's page clicked from 1,243 to 1,244. Someone was there. The computer voice announced: "You have a visitor." Fi stirred slightly in her sleep as a message window popped up on the screen to tell her she was receiving a file via e-mail. When the transmission completed, the computer turned itself off. The cover closed itself slowly and snapped shut although there was no one there to touch it. The room was in darkness once again.

Fi's So Weird Web page had just gotten a whole lot weirder.